PJMASKS
Gekko Saves Christmas

Based on the episode "Gekko Saves Christmas"

SIMON SPOTLIGHT
An imprint of Simon & Schuster Children's Publishing Division
New York   London   Toronto   Sydney   New Delhi
1230 Avenue of the Americas, New York, New York 10020
This Simon Spotlight edition September 2017
This book is based on the TV series PJ Masks © Frog Box / Entertainment One UK Limited / Walt Disney EMEA Productions Limited 2014;
Les Pyjamasques by Romauld © (2007) Gallimard Jeunesse. All Rights Reserved. This book/publication © Entertainment One UK Limited 2017.
Adapted by Maggie Testa from the series PJ Masks. All rights reserved, including the right of reproduction in whole or in part in any form.
SIMON SPOTLIGHT and colophon are registered trademarks of Simon & Schuster, Inc. For information about special discounts for bulk purchases,
please contact Simon & Schuster Special Sales at 1-866-506-1949 or business@simonandschuster.com.
Manufactured in the United States of America 0817 LAK
2 4 6 8 10 9 7 5 3 1
ISBN 978-1-5344-0150-1 (pbk) • ISBN 978-1-5344-0151-8 (eBook)

It's Christmas Eve, and Connor, Greg, and Amaya are ice-skating. Well, sort of. As Amaya and Connor glide along the ice, Greg slips and slides and crashes into a wall.

"I'm not any good at this," he groans.

"We'll help you," says Connor. "Just try. Skating is part of Christmas, like the tree!"

Amaya nods. "Yeah! With all its lights and decorations!"

"What lights and decorations?" asks Greg.

Amaya and Connor look up at the tree. It's bare! Even the star at the top is gone.

This is a job for the PJ Masks!

"PJ Masks, we're on our way! Into the night to save the day!"
Connor becomes Catboy!
Amaya becomes Owlette!
Greg becomes Gekko!

"Whoever took those decorations went really high. We need to get up high too!" says Catboy at headquarters.

"To the Owl-Glider!" says Owlette.

Up in the Owl-Glider, the heroes spot Luna Girl in the sky.

"Gasping Gekkos! She's taking everyone's presents with her Luna Magnet," says Gekko. "If we could get her Luna Board, she wouldn't be able to reach the chimneys."

"Good idea, Gekko," says Catboy. "Let's go!"

Owlette pushes a button on the Owl-Glider, and a gust of wind forces Luna Girl off her Luna Board. Catboy jumps out of the Owl-Glider and chases Luna Girl.

Owlette runs to grab the Luna Board, but Luna Girl summons her moths.

"Owlette! Look out!" shouts Gekko, but it's too late. The moths catch Owlette.

"Quick, Gekko," she says, "fly the Luna Board away from Luna Girl!"

Gekko is nervous. "I've never ridden a Luna Board before," he says, climbing on. "I won't be able to do it."

The Luna Board slips out from under Gekko's feet and goes flying right to Luna Girl!

"So long, kitty!" Luna Girl says to Catboy. "I'm *meowwt* of here!"

The moths let go of Owlette, and the heroes meet up with one another.

"Gekko, are you okay?" asks Catboy.

"Yes," says Gekko, "but I knew I wouldn't be able to fly the Luna Board. Sorry."

"It's okay," says Catboy. "Let's just go after Luna Girl. Owlette, you fly, and we'll follow you from the ground."

Owlette soon catches up with Luna Girl. "Why don't you just give those presents back?" Owlette asks.

"Because I don't want to!" replies Luna Girl. "Come and get them if you think you can!"

Owlette rushes at Luna Girl, but Luna Girl is ready for her. She uses her Luna Magnet to stop Owlette!

"Super Cat Jump!" Catboy yells as he races off to help Owlette. He grabs onto the Luna Board. As Luna Girl tries to shake him off, she lets go of the Luna Magnet. Owlette is free, but now she is falling through the air!

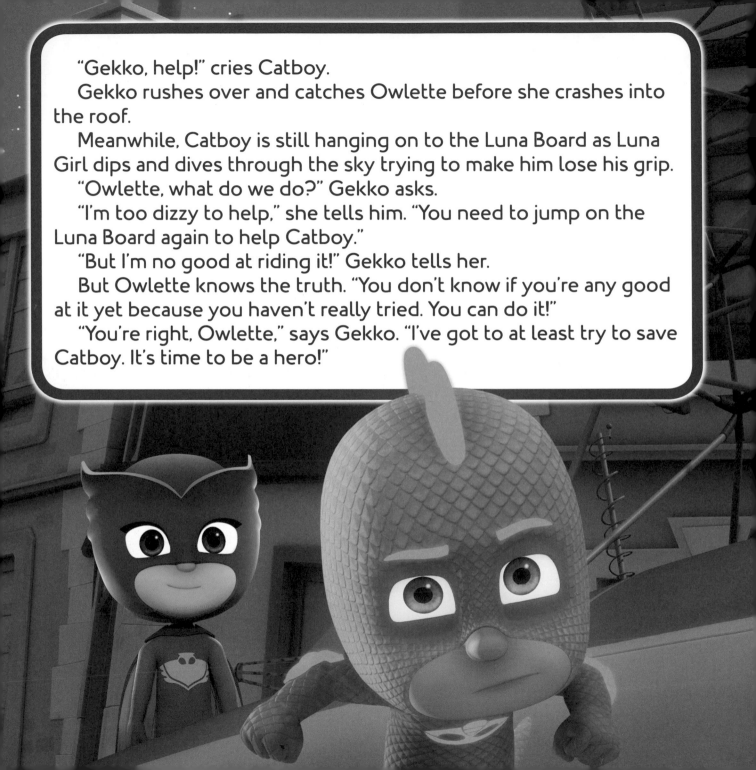

"Gekko, help!" cries Catboy.

Gekko rushes over and catches Owlette before she crashes into the roof.

Meanwhile, Catboy is still hanging on to the Luna Board as Luna Girl dips and dives through the sky trying to make him lose his grip.

"Owlette, what do we do?" Gekko asks.

"I'm too dizzy to help," she tells him. "You need to jump on the Luna Board again to help Catboy."

"But I'm no good at riding it!" Gekko tells her.

But Owlette knows the truth. "You don't know if you're any good at it yet because you haven't really tried. You can do it!"

"You're right, Owlette," says Gekko. "I've got to at least try to save Catboy. It's time to be a hero!"

"Super Gekko Camouflage!" Gekko cries as he runs up a building. Luna Girl and Catboy whiz by on the Luna Board. Gekko jumps . . . and lands right next to Luna Girl.

Luna Girl is so surprised that she falls off the Luna Board and lands on the roof.

Gekko and Catboy are still on the Luna Board. Gekko swerves as he gets used to flying it.

"Don't panic, Gekko, or we'll crash," Catboy tells him.

"Right," says Gekko. "Careful. I'll just bring it down slowly."

Gekko makes a smooth landing on the roof. He and Catboy are safe!

"Way to go," says Catboy, "I knew you'd get the hang of it. You just had to give it a try!"

Gekko turns to Luna Girl. "It's over," he says. "We've got your Luna Board so you can't steal any more presents!"

Luna Girl frowns. "It's not fair! I never get a real Christmas. I'm just here by myself."

That gives Gekko an idea. "Why don't you spend the rest of Christmas Eve with us? We've got to put all these presents and decorations back anyway. You can help."

"Then we'll all have Christmas together," says Catboy. "What do you say?"

"Okay, I guess," says Luna Girl.

Gekko stands on the Luna Board again. "Then hop on! We're going to save Christmas!"

Together, the PJ Masks and Luna Girl go from chimney to chimney returning Christmas presents. They even decorate the Christmas tree again.

"Isn't it beautiful, Luna Girl?" Gekko asks.

"I guess," Luna Girl replies. "But now Christmas really is over, and I didn't get any presents."

"Oh, yes you did!" Catboy tells her.
The PJ Masks have a present for Luna Girl!
Luna Girl opens the box.
"Ice skates!" she says. "But I've never skated before."
"That's okay," says Gekko. "Neither have I, but we'll get the hang of it. Come on, let's just try!"

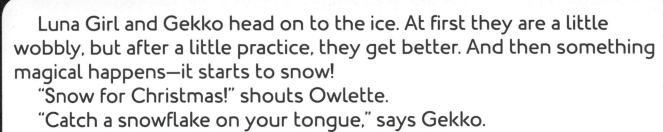

Luna Girl and Gekko head on to the ice. At first they are a little wobbly, but after a little practice, they get better. And then something magical happens—it starts to snow!

"Snow for Christmas!" shouts Owlette.

"Catch a snowflake on your tongue," says Gekko.

PJ Masks all shout hooray! 'Cause on Christmas Eve, we saved Christmas day! Merry Christmas, everyone!